THE BARK PARK

by Lori Haskins Houran
illustrated by John Joven

KANEPRESS

AN IMPRINT OF ASTRA BOOKS FOR YOUNG READERS
New York

For Coco and Bailey—L.H.H.

To Avril, Ian, and Ana. You complete my life 100%.
—J.J.

Copyright © 2022 by Astra Publishing House
All rights reserved. Copying or digitizing this book for storage, display, or distribution
in any other medium is strictly prohibited. For information regarding permission,
contact the publisher through its website: astrapublishinghouse.com.

Kane Press
An imprint of Astra Books for Young Readers, a division of Astra Publishing House
astrapublishinghouse.com

Printed in China

Library of Congress Cataloging-in-Publication Data

Names: Houran, Lori Haskins, author. | Joven, John, illustrator.
Title: The bark park / by Lori Haskins Houran ; illustrated by John Joven.
Description: First edition. | New York : Kane Press, an imprint of Astra
Publishing House, [2022] | Series: Math matters | Audience: Ages 5-8. |
Summary: Lila and her friends are troubled when they discover the dog
park does not have a bench for eighty-year-old Mr. Romero to use, so
they decide to start a dog-wash to raise money for one, and learn about
percentages along the way.
Identifiers: LCCN 2021036018 (print) | LCCN 2021036019 (ebook) |
ISBN 9781635925425 (paperback) | ISBN 9781635925432 (ebook)
Subjects: LCSH: Parks for dogs—Juvenile fiction. | Money-making projects
for children—Juvenile fiction. | Percentage—Juvenile fiction. |
Mathematics—Juvenile fiction. | CYAC: Moneymaking projects—Fiction. |
Parks—Fiction. | Mathematics—Fiction. | LCGFT: Picture books.
Classification: LCC PZ7.H27645 Bar 2022 (print) | LCC PZ7.H27645 (ebook)
| DDC [E]—dc23
LC record available at https://lccn.loc.gov/2021036018
LC ebook record available at https://lccn.loc.gov/2021036019

10 9 8 7 6 5 4 3 2 1

Math Matters® is a registered trademark of Astra Publishing House.

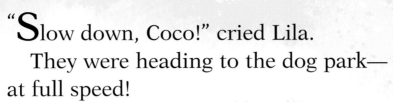

"Slow down, Coco!" cried Lila.
They were heading to the dog park—
at full speed!

3

Suddenly, Coco screeched to a stop.

"*Arf! Arf!*" She barked hello to the neighbor's dog, Lady.

Lila took a second to catch her breath.

"Hi, Mr. Romero," she said. "We're going to the Bark Park. Want to come?"

"Oh, Lady loves it there," said Mr. Romero.
"But there's no place to sit down, and my legs
get tired. I turn eighty on Monday, you know."
"Wow," said Lila. "Happy almost birthday!"
Coco started tugging again.
"Oops. Gotta go!"

At the Bark Park, Lila let Coco off her leash. Coco ran around with the other dogs, wagging her tail.

Lila kept thinking about Lady. Too bad she couldn't play here, too.

A small dog bounded into the park with Lila's friend Nolan and his big sister Sophie.

"Hi, Lila!" Nolan said. "How are things?"

Just like that, the whole story of Mr. Romero and Lady poured out. "The town should put a bench here," Lila said.

"Yeah!" said Sophie. "Our mom is on the park committee. I'll call her right now!"

Sophie hung up. She was frowning. "Mom thinks it's a great idea. But there's no money for a bench."

"How much do they cost?" Lila asked.

Sophie searched on her phone. "Here's one for two hundred dollars. No, wait—it's fifty percent off. That's half the price. *One* hundred dollars."

"Yikes!" said Nolan. "It's still a lot of money!"

"What if we had a bake sale?" said
Lila. "Or a car wash. Or—"
"BITSY! STOP IT!"
A lady rushed over to a tiny poodle.
Bitsy was rolling around on the ground.
Her curly fur was caked with mud.

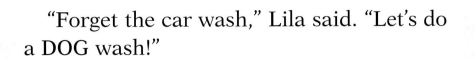

"Forget the car wash," Lila said. "Let's do a DOG wash!"

Everything fell into place.

The park committee said yes to the dog wash. Lila's parents offered dog shampoo, buckets, and old towels.

On Saturday morning, Nolan made a sign.
DOG WASH TODAY!

They charged $5 a dog.

Sophie drew a chart with their goal at the top. They had to earn $100.

Some of the jobs were easy.
Others . . . not so much.

After an hour, the kids were dripping wet.
But they had made twenty-five dollars.

Sophie colored in the bottom of the chart. "We're at twenty-five percent already!"

"We only made twenty-five cents?" Nolan yelped.

"No, twenty-five *percent*," said Sophie. "Percent means how much you have out of one hundred."

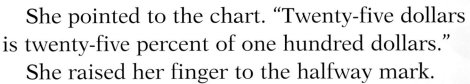

She pointed to the chart. "Twenty-five dollars is twenty-five percent of one hundred dollars."

She raised her finger to the halfway mark. "Fifty dollars would be . . ."

"Fifty percent?" guessed Lila.

"Right!" said Sophie.

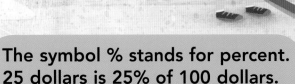

The symbol % stands for percent. 25 dollars is 25% of 100 dollars.

The kids scrubbed and rinsed. They washed big dogs and small dogs. Fluffy dogs and sleek dogs.

They even washed a pet that *wasn't* a dog!

By noon, they had hit fifty percent of their goal.

50 dollars is 50% of 100 dollars.

By one o'clock, they had earned seventy-five dollars. That was seventy-five percent of their goal. They were going to make it!

Lila smiled. She couldn't wait to bring Mr. Romero and Lady to the park on Monday. The bench would be a *perfect* birthday surprise.

75 dollars is 75% of 100 dollars.

Then Lila felt something. A raindrop. *Two* raindrops.

She looked up. The sky was black. Rain started pouring down!

"Eeeeeek!" People raced out of the park, tugging their dogs behind them.

Soon the Bark Park was empty, except for three glum kids.

Sophie grabbed the soggy sign. Lila and Nolan picked up the buckets, shampoo, and towels.

They trudged out of the Bark Park.

Goal!

100%

75%

50%

25%

"YOO-HOO! YOOOOO-HOO!"

Bitsy's owner was calling to them from a house across the street. "I was on my way to the park when it started to rain! Can you do a dog wash here, in my garage?"

The kids looked at each other.

"We still need twenty-five dollars. Washing one dog is only five dollars," said Nolan.

"But Bitsy really needs a bath," Lila said.

They crossed the street.

"Thanks, kids. Bitsy is awfully muddy.
So are her puppies." The lady let out a whistle.
Four more poodles ran into the garage!
"Twenty-five dollars, right?" the lady said.
Lila couldn't believe it!

They broke out the dog shampoo again. Soon, five very dirty poodles were squeaky clean.

100 dollars is 100% of 100 dollars.

"We did it," Lila said. "One hundred dollars!"
"That's one hundred percent!" said Sophie.
Lila colored in the chart—all the way to the top.

On Monday, the grass in the Bark Park was extra green from Saturday's rain. The new yellow bench shone in the sun.

Lila led Mr. Romero to it. "You can open your eyes now," she said.

"SURPRISE!" the kids shouted.

"Oh, my word!" Mr. Romero sat right
down on the bench. "Now isn't this comfy!
And look how happy Lady is, playing
with her friends."

Mr. Romero leaned back on the bench. "In all my eighty years, this is the best birthday surprise I ever had."

"Really?" Lila said.

"Yes," said Mr. Romero. "One hundred percent!"

COMPARING GOALS

Woof! Time to fix up more bark parks for Coco and Lady! Sophie and Nolan made charts to keep track of the progress toward their goals.

Coco   **Lady**

- Which chart shows percentages?
- Which chart shows dollars?
- What does the 50 on each chart represent?
- Can you tell who has raised more money?